W9-CAI-451

The Velveteen Rabbit

Or
How Toys Become Real

Margery Williams

Illustrations by William Nicholson

Health Communications, Inc.
Deerfield Beach, Florida

www.hcibooks.com

Library of Congress Cataloging-in-Publication Data
is available through the Library of Congress.

© Margery Williams

ISBN-13: 978-0-7573-0333-3
ISBN-10: 0-7573-0333-1

Publisher: Health Communications, Inc.
            3201 S.W. 15th Street
            Deerfield Beach, FL 33442-8190

Cover design by Larissa Hise Henoch
Inside book design by Lawna Patterson Oldfield

Foreword

My parents were not readers, and this classic book—*The Velveteen Rabbit*—had not been part of my childhood. I was not raised to value my individuality and accept, even treasure, my imperfections. Instead I spent much of my life hating those parts of me that were "different." Then I had children of my own and found I loved everything about them, including their foibles and flaws. And they opened my heart to the idea that I was okay too, even if others found things about me to criticize.

In this way, my daughters prepared me for Margery Williams's beautiful story, which offers wisdom far beyond what you might expect from an illustrated children's book. By the time this little book found its way into my life, I was ready to consider its main message—that we all have a place in life and deserve love and respect.

The beauty of *The Velveteen Rabbit* comes over you slowly, the way a sunrise brings a breathtaking landscape into view. The first sign comes with the introduction of the lonely Rabbit him-self. The cold attitudes voiced by some toys in the nursery where the Rabbit lives make you worry about his fate. But then the Skin Horse appears and you begin to feel like everything is going to be all right. You rejoice when the Boy learns to love the Rabbit, and you feel sorry for him when the other rabbits reveal to him his so-called "imperfections." You begin to truly care for this stuffed bunny. You long for him to complete his journey to Real, because in a way you feel he is undertaking the journey for all of us.

It may seem strange to talk about an old fashioned children's velveteen bunny this way. Who, after all, would invest such interest and empathy in children's toys?

Well, it turns out that Margery Williams would. As a child her own toys were as real to her as any human being. Later in life Williams still held stuffed animals, dolls, and other toys in high regard. "By thinking about toys and remembering toys, they suddenly become very much alive," she said when she was in middle age.

The sensitivity and skill Margery Williams shows as a writer hints at the wistful loneliness in her childhood. Raised in London and then New York, she attended school for a just few years. The rest of the time she was educated alone, at home. The tutoring allowed this extraordinarily bright young woman to make quick progress, and by the time she was seventeen she was a published author.

While she sometimes wrote for adults, Williams's best and most memorable works were for children and she considered this genre the most demanding. "Nothing is easier than to write a story for children," she once quipped, "few things are harder, as any writer knows, than to achieve a story that children will really like."

◆◆◆

The Velveteen Rabbit, which first appeared in 1922, is full of the magic and playfulness that fill a child's world and are almost impossible to find in the land of adults.

But as many millions of readers have discovered, this book offers wisdom for readers of all ages. The story confronts some of the most essential questions we ever ask: Who am I? Do I have worth? What is life all about?

As they search for happiness, each one of Williams's characters seems to embody very basic human traits. The Rabbit is that part of us who is young at heart, and hopeful, and insecure, and afraid. The not-so-nice toys in the nursery represent excessive pride, superiority and insensitive competitiveness. Nana, the governess, is cold and too busy to notice much about others. And the Skin Horse stands for the kindness, wisdom and quiet integrity we all hope to acquire some day.

Yes, it is a story for children. But it is also meant for any person with an open mind and a receptive heart. As you read this wonderful book, the genuine humanity in its characters will become obvious. You will begin to consider how much you are like the little Rabbit, and how much you admire the Skin Horse. Most important, you will begin to understand that by holding true to your highest values, and honoring your own life's experience, you too can strive to be Real, just like the Horse and the Rabbit.

◆◆◆

I can make a good guess about how you will be affected by *The Velveteen Rabbit* because I have felt this book's subtle power. I was so moved the first time I read it to my young daughters that I began a long reassessment of my values and how I viewed myself. This didn't happen in a fully conscious way. I just found myself wondering, like the Rabbit, "What is Real?"

Months passed before I fully understood the key messages Margery Williams offers: that we all deserve to be loved, that our real worth is in our hearts and our spirits, and that our value has nothing to do with how we look or what we own. After I took time to figure these things out, I gradually experienced an awakening. I began to let go of my self-critical impulses. And I found myself looking for moments when people around me acted in loving and authentic ways. They happened more often, and in more places, than I expected.

It would take me about ten more years to transform the wisdom I found in *The Velveteen Rabbit* into a series of ideals—

principles really—the helped to guide my life. Much of this process occurred in my work as a psychotherapist. Time and again I saw how my clients had been terribly hurt by the loss of their Real selves and how they were healed when they began to recover it.

In the first years of working with this book I did not tell my colleagues that one of the most influential works on my office shelves was a parable about a toy Rabbit in a child's nursery. Similarly, many people who read *The Velveteen Rabbit* as adults are shy about admitting that it touched them so deeply. But in fact, more than sixty years after her death, Margery Williams's work continues to have a profound effect on new readers. This became obvious to me after the publication of my book, *The Velveteen Principles,* which honors her original ideals and uses them as a base for exploring how we might lead Real lives in today's too-often harsh and competitive world.

Time and again, as I meet people who have read my book, I discover they are members of a vast secret society of people who cherish *The Velveteen Rabbit.* They say, "Oh yes, I remember that book, I wish I had it to read now." Or they say, "I think my copy is in my attic somewhere; I'm going to go get it right away!"

Days after the first copies of *The Velveteen Principles* arrived at my house, fresh from the printer, I left one on the porch at my neighbor's house. Later she came across the street to thank me for the gift and to explain how much the original *Velveteen Rabbit* had meant to her.

"I read *The Velveteen Rabbit* to my daughter and we both still love it," she said. "But I didn't know other people felt this way."

My neighbor made me realize that there might be many people who value the lessons in *The Velveteen Rabbit* but don't say so because they don't want to be judged negatively. (Critical people might say it's a simple children's story, not worth all the fuss.) I hope you will not be shy in this way. One of the greatest lessons of Margery Williams's life is that when we say something heartfelt, kind people respond. If you doubt this is true, consider how the world responded to Miss Williams's little book. It sold millions of copies, many of which became prized possessions handed from one generation to the next.

Margery Williams proved that when we tell the truth about what we value, we also allow others to join us, to appreciate us, and affirm us. I know, because it happens in my own life, and it happens in the community forums on the Web site established to support my book. At *www.velveteenprinciples.com* readers offer genuine, compassionate and thoughtful responses to those who are open about their own struggle to be Real. This is how one forum writer named Amy put it:

"We all have our own hopes, dreams, passions, and desires. Nobody should feel ashamed to be different. If everybody were the same, what a boring place the world would be."

Another member of the Web site forum, Gerry, helped us all understand how he interprets Margery Williams's notions about the value of being Real.

"Even the word flaw gives a negative connotation. Idiosyncrasies and quirks work better. I like to think of them as uniquenesses."

Those of us who trade experiences and insights on the Internet are not the only ones who feel inspired by Margery Williams and the Real ideal. I know teachers use her book in classrooms and even college lecture halls. Truly a classic, the book has been adapted as a stage play, a ballet and even recorded onto a compact disc.

The music, literature and acts of grace inspired by *The Velveteen Rabbit* make up a grand testament to Margery Williams. And more than eighty years after it was first published, the book still makes its most important mark one reader at a time. But don't take my word for it. Let yourself get lost in the Velveteen Rabbit's world for a few moments. When you've turned the last page, you'll feel it in your heart.

Toni Raiten-D'Antonio
Author, *The Velveteen Principles:*
A Guide to Becoming Real

HERE was once
a velveteen rabbit,
and in the beginning
he was really
splendid.

He was fat and bunchy, as a rabbit should be; his coat was spotted brown and white, he had real thread whiskers, and his ears were lined with pink sateen. On Christmas morning, when he sat wedged in the top of the Boy's stocking, with a sprig of holly between his paws, the effect was charming.

There were other things in the stocking, nuts and oranges and a toy engine, and chocolate almonds and a clockwork mouse, but the Rabbit was quite the best of all. For at least two hours the Boy loved him, and then Aunts and Uncles came to dinner, and there was a great rustling of tissue paper and unwrapping of parcels, and in the excitement of looking at all the new presents the Velveteen Rabbit was forgotten.

For a long time he lived
in the toy cupboard or on the
nursery floor, and no one
thought very much about him.
He was naturally shy, and being
only made of velveteen, some of
the more expensive toys quite
snubbed him. The mechanical
toys were very superior,
and looked down upon every
one else; they were full of
modern ideas, and pretended
they were real.

The model boat,
who had lived through two
seasons and lost most of his
paint, caught the tone from
them and never missed an
opportunity of referring to his
rigging in technical terms.
The Rabbit could not claim
to be a model of anything,

for he didn't know that
real rabbits existed; he thought
they were all stuffed with
sawdust like himself, and he
understood that sawdust was
quite out-of-date and should
never be mentioned in
modern circles.

ven Timothy, the jointed wooden lion, who was made by the disabled soldiers, and should have had broader views, put on airs and pretended he was connected with Government. Between them all the poor little Rabbit was made to feel himself very insignificant and commonplace, and the only person who was kind to him at all was the Skin Horse.

The Skin Horse
had lived longer in the
nursery than any of the others.
He was so old that his brown
coat was bald in patches
and showed the seams
underneath, and most of the
hairs in his tail had been
pulled out to string
bead necklaces.

He was wise, for he had seen a long succession of mechanical toys arrive to boast and swagger, and by-and-by break their mainsprings and pass away, and he knew that they were only toys, and would never turn into anything else. For nursery magic is very strange and wonderful, and only those playthings that are old and wise and experienced like the Skin Horse understand all about it.

"What is REAL?" asked the Rabbit one day, when they were lying side by side near the nursery fender, before Nana came to tidy the room. "Does it mean having things that buzz inside you and a stick-out handle?"

"Real isn't how you are made," said the Skin Horse. "It's a thing that happens to you. When a child loves you for a long, long time, not just to play with, but REALLY loves you, then you become Real."

"Does it hurt?"
asked the Rabbit.
"Sometimes," said the
Skin Horse, for he was
always truthful.
"When you are Real you don't
mind being hurt."

"Does it happen all
at once, like being wound up,"
he asked, "or bit by bit?"
"It doesn't happen all at once,"
said the Skin Horse.
"You become. It takes a
long time. That's why it
doesn't happen often to people
who break easily, or have
sharp edges, or who have
to be carefully kept.

Generally, by the time you
are Real, most of your hair has
been loved off, and your eyes
drop out and you get loose in
your joints and very shabby.
But these things don't matter
at all, because once you
are Real you can't be ugly,
except to people who
don't understand."

"I suppose *you* are real?" said the Rabbit. And then he wished he had not said it, for he thought the Skin Horse might be sensitive. But the Skin Horse only smiled. "The Boy's Uncle made me Real," he said. "That was a great many years ago; but once you are Real you can't become unreal again. It lasts for always."

The Rabbit sighed.
He thought it would be a
long time before this magic
called Real happened to him.
He longed to become Real,
to know what it felt like;
and yet the idea of growing
shabby and losing his eyes and
whiskers was rather sad.
He wished that he could
become it without these
uncomfortable things
happening to him.

There was a person called
Nana who ruled the nursery.
Sometimes she took no notice of
the playthings lying about,
and sometimes, for no reason
whatever, she went swooping
about like a great wind and
hustled them away in cupboards.
She called this "tidying up,"
and the playthings all hated it,
especially the tin ones.
The Rabbit didn't mind it so
much, for wherever he was
thrown he came down soft.

One evening, when the
Boy was going to bed,
he couldn't find the china dog
that always slept with him.
Nana was in a hurry, and it was
too much trouble to hunt
for china dogs at bedtime,
so she simply looked about her,
and seeing that the toy cupboard
stood open, she made a swoop.
"Here," she said, "take your
old Bunny! He'll do to sleep with
you!" And she dragged the
Rabbit out by one ear, and put
him into the Boy's arms.

That night, and for many nights after, the Velveteen Rabbit slept in the Boy's bed. At first he found it uncomfortable, for the Boy hugged him very tight, and sometimes he rolled over on him, and sometimes he pushed him so far under the pillow that the Rabbit could scarcely breathe. And he missed, too, those long moonlight hours in the nursery, when all the house was silent, and his talks with the Skin Horse.

But very soon
he grew to like it, for the
Boy used to talk to him, and
made nice tunnels for him
under the bedclothes that he
said were like the burrow
the real rabbits lived in.
And they had splendid
games together, in whispers,
when Nana had gone
away to her

supper and left the
night-light burning on
the mantelpiece.
And when the Boy dropped
off to sleep, the Rabbit
would snuggle down close
under his little warm chin
and dream, with the
Boy's hands clasped close
round him all
night long.

And so time went on,
and the little Rabbit was very
happy—so happy that he
never noticed how his beautiful
velveteen fur was getting
shabbier and shabbier, and
his tail becoming unsewn,
and all the pink rubbed off
his nose where the Boy
had kissed him.

Spring came, and
they had long days in the
garden, for wherever the Boy
went the Rabbit went too.
He had rides in the
wheelbarrow, and picnics
on the grass, and lovely
fairy huts built for him under
the raspberry canes behind
the flower border.

And once, when the Boy was called away suddenly to go to tea, the Rabbit was left out on the lawn until long after dusk, and Nana had to come and look for him with the candle because the Boy couldn't go to sleep unless he was there. He was wet through with the dew and quite earthy from diving into the burrows the Boy had made for him in the flower bed, and Nana grumbled as she rubbed him off with a corner of her apron.

"You must have your
old Bunny!" she said.
"Fancy all that fuss for a toy!"
"Give me my Bunny!" he said.
"You mustn't say that. He isn't a
toy. He's REAL!" When the little
Rabbit heard that he was happy,
for he knew what the Skin Horse
had said was true at last.
The nursery magic had
happened to him, and he was
a toy no longer. He was Real.
The Boy himself
had said it.

That night he was almost
too happy to sleep, and so much
love stirred in his little sawdust
heart that it almost burst.
And into his boot-button eyes,
that had long ago lost their
polish, there came a look of
wisdom and beauty, so that
even Nana noticed it next
morning when she picked him
up, and said, "I declare if that
old Bunny hasn't got quite
a knowing expression!"

hat was
a wonderful Summer!

Near the house where they lived there was a wood, and in the long June evening the Boy liked to go there after tea to play. He took the Velveteen Rabbit with him, and before he wandered off to pick flowers, or play at brigands among the trees, he always made the Rabbit a little nest somewhere among the bracken, where he would be quite cosy, for he was a kind-hearted little boy and he liked Bunny to be comfortable.

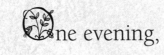One evening,
while the Rabbit was
lying there alone, watching
the ants that ran to and fro
between his velvet paws
in the grass, he saw two strange
beings creep out of the tall
bracken near him.

They were rabbits
like himself, but quite furry
and brand-new. They must have
been very well made, for their
seams didn't show at all,
and they changed shape in a
queer way when they moved;
one minute they were long
and thin and the next minute
fat and bunchy, instead of
always staying the same
like he did.

Their feet padded softly on the ground, and they crept quite close to him, twitching their noses, while the Rabbit stared hard to see which side the clockwork stuck out, for he knew that people who jump generally have something to wind them up. But he couldn't see it. They were evidently a new kind of rabbit altogether.

They stared
at him, and the little
Rabbit stared back.
And all the time
their noses
twitched.

"Why don't you
get up and play with us?"
one of them asked.
"I don't feel like it," said the
Rabbit, for he didn't want
to explain that he had
no clockwork.
"Ho!" said the furry rabbit.
"It's as easy as anything,"
And he gave a big hop
sideways and stood
on his hind legs.

"I don't believe you can!"
he said.
"I can!" said the little Rabbit.
"I can jump higher than
anything." He meant when
the Boy threw him,
but of course he didn't
want to say so.
"Can you hop on your
hind legs?" asked the
furry rabbit.

That was a
dreadful question, for
the Velveteen Rabbit had
no hind legs at all!
The back of him was
made all in one piece,
like a pincushion.
He sat still in the bracken,
and hoped that the other
rabbit wouldn't notice.
"I don't want to!"
he said again.

But the wild rabbits
have very sharp eyes.
And this one stretched out
his neck and looked.
"He hasn't got any hind legs!"
he called out. "Fancy a
rabbit without any hind legs!"
And he began to laugh.
"I have!" cried the little Rabbit.
"I have got hind legs! I am
sitting on them!"

"Then stretch them out
and show me, like this!"
said the wild rabbit.
And he began to whirl round
and dance, till the little
Rabbit got quite dizzy.
"I don't like dancing,"
he said.
"I'd rather sit still!"

$\mathcal{B}$ut all the while
he was longing to dance,
for a funny new tickly feeling
ran through him, and he felt
he would give anything
in the world to be able
to jump about like these
rabbits did.

The strange rabbit stopped
dancing, and came quite close.
He came so close this time that
his long whiskers brushed the
Velveteen Rabbit's ear, and then
he wrinkled his nose suddenly
and flattened his ears and
jumped backwards.
"He doesn't smell right!"
he exclaimed. "He isn't a rabbit
at all! He isn't real!"
"I *am* Real!" said the little Rabbit.
"I am Real! The Boy said so!"
And he nearly began to cry.

Just then there was
a sound of footsteps, and
the Boy ran past near them,
and with a stamp of feet and
a flash of white tails the two
strange rabbits disappeared.
"Come back and play with me!"
called the little Rabbit.
"Oh, do come back!
I *know* I am Real!"

But there was
no answer, only the little
ants ran to and fro, and the
bracken swayed gently where
the two strangers had passed.
The Velveteen Rabbit
was all alone.
"Oh, dear!" he thought.
"Why did they run away
like that?
Why couldn't they stop
and talk to me?"

For a long time
he lay very still, watching
the bracken, and hoping that
they would come back.
But they never returned, and
presently the sun sank lower
and the little white moths
fluttered out, and the Boy
came and carried
him home.

eeks passed,
and the little Rabbit
grew very old and shabby,
but the Boy loved him
just as much.

He loved him so hard that he loved all his whiskers off, and the pink lining to his ears turned grey, and his brown spots faded. He even began to lose his shape, and he scarcely looked like a rabbit any more, except to the Boy. To him he was always beautiful, and that was all that the little Rabbit cared about. He didn't mind how he looked to other people, because the nursery magic had made him Real, and when you are Real shabbiness doesn't matter.

And then, one day,
the Boy was ill.
His face grew very flushed,
and he talked in his sleep,
and his little body was
so hot that it burned the
Rabbit when he held
him close.

Strange people came
and went in the nursery,
and a light burned all night and
through it all the little Velveteen
Rabbit lay there, hidden from
sight under the bedclothes,
and he never stirred, for
he was afraid that if they found
him some one might take
him away, and he knew that
the Boy needed him.

It was a long weary time,
for the Boy was too ill to play,
and the little Rabbit found
it rather dull with nothing
to do all day long.
But he snuggled down
patiently, and looked forward
to the time when the Boy
should be well again,
and they would go out
in the garden amongst
the flowers and the

butterflies and play
splendid games in the
raspberry thicket like
they used to.
All sorts of delightful
things he planned, and
while the Boy lay half asleep
he crept up close to the
pillow and whispered
them in his ear.

And presently
the fever turned, and
the Boy got better.
He was able to sit up
in bed and look at
picture-books, while the
little Rabbit cuddled close
at his side. And one day,
they let him get up
and dress.

It was a bright,
sunny morning, and the
windows stood wide open.
They had carried the
Boy out on the balcony,
wrapped in a shawl, and
the little Rabbit lay
tangled up among
the bedclothes,
thinking.

The Boy was going
to the seaside to-morrow.
Everything was arranged, and
now it only remained to carry
out the doctor's orders.
They talked about it all,
while the little Rabbit lay under
the bedclothes, with just his
head peeping out, and listened.
The room was to be disinfected,
and all the books and toys
that the Boy had played with
in bed must be burnt.

"Hurrah!"
thought the little Rabbit.
"To-morrow we shall go to
the seaside!" For the Boy had
often talked of the seaside,
and he wanted very much to
see the big waves coming in,
and the tiny crabs, and
the sand castles.
Just then Nana caught
sight of him. "How about
his old Bunny?"
she asked.

"*That?*" said the doctor.
"Why, it's a mass of scarlet fever
germs!—Burn it at once.
What? Nonsense!
Get him a new one.
He mustn't have that any more!"
And so the little Rabbit
was put into a sack with the
old picture-books and
a lot of rubbish, and carried
out to the end of the
garden behind

the fowl-house.
That was a fine place
to make a bonfire, only
the gardener was too busy
just then to attend to it.
He had the potatoes
to dig and the green peas
to gather, but next morning
he promised to come
quite early and burn
the whole lot.

That night the Boy
slept in a different bedroom,
and he had a new bunny to
sleep with him. It was a
splendid bunny, all white plush
with real glass eyes, but the
Boy was too excited to care
very much about it.
For to-morrow he was going
to the seaside, and that in
itself was such a wonderful
thing that he could think
of nothing else.

And while the Boy
was asleep, dreaming of the
seaside, the little Rabbit
lay among the old picture-books
in the corner behind the
fowl-house, and he felt very
lonely. The sack had been left
untied, and so by wriggling a
bit he was able to get his head
through the opening and look
out. He was shivering a little,
for he had always been used

to sleeping in a proper bed,
and by this time his coat
had worn so thin and
threadbare from hugging that
it was no longer any protection
to him. Near by he could see
the thicket of raspberry canes,
growing tall and close like a
tropical jungle, in whose
shadow he had played with
the Boy on bygone
mornings.

He thought of those long sunlit hours in the garden—how happy they were—and a great sadness came over him. He seemed to see them all pass before him, each more beautiful than the other, the fairy huts in the flower-bed, the quiet evenings in the wood when he lay in the bracken and the little ants ran over his paws; the wonderful day when he first knew that he was Real. He thought of the Skin Horse, so wise and gentle, and all that he had told him.

Of what use was it
to be loved and lose one's
beauty and become Real
if it all ended like this?
And a tear, a real tear,
trickled down his little
shabby velvet nose and
fell to the ground.

And then a strange thing happened. For where the tear had fallen a flower grew out of the ground, a mysterious flower, not at all like any that grew in the garden. It had slender green leaves the colour of emeralds, and in the centre of the leaves a blossom like a golden cup. It was so beautiful that the little Rabbit forgot to cry, and just lay there watching it. And presently the blossom opened, and out of it there stepped a fairy.

She was quite the loveliest fairy in the whole world. Her dress was of pearl and dew-drops, and there were flowers round her neck and in her hair, and her face was like the most perfect flower of all. And she came close to the little Rabbit and gathered him up in her arms and kissed him on his velveteen nose that was all damp from crying.

"Little Rabbit," she said, "don't you know who I am?"

The Rabbit looked up
at her, and it seemed to him
that he had seen her face before,
but he couldn't think where.
"I am the nursery magic Fairy,"
she said. "I take care of all
the playthings that the children
have loved. When they are
old and worn out, and the
children don't need them any
more, then I come and take
them away with me and
turn them into Real."

"Wasn't I Real before?"
asked the little Rabbit.
"You were Real to the Boy,"
the Fairy said,
"because he loved you.
Now you shall be Real
to every one."

And she held the little Rabbit close in her arms and flew with him into the wood. It was light now, for the moon had risen. All the forest was beautiful, and the fronds of the bracken shone like frosted silver. In the open glade between the tree-trunks the wild rabbits danced with their shadows on the velvet grass, but when they saw the Fairy they all stopped dancing and stood round in a ring to stare at her.

"I've brought you a
new playfellow," the Fairy said.
"You must be very kind to
him and teach him all he needs
to know in Rabbit-land,
for he is going to live with
you for ever and ever!"
And she kissed the little
Rabbit again and put him
down on the grass.
"Run and play, little Rabbit!"
she said.

But the little Rabbit
sat quite still for a moment
and never moved.
For when he saw all the
wild rabbits dancing around
him he suddenly remembered
about his hind legs, and he
didn't want them to see
that he was made all
in one piece.

He did not know that
when the Fairy kissed him
that last time she had changed
him altogether. And he might
have sat there a long time,
too shy to move,
if just then something
hadn't tickled his nose, and
before he thought what he
was doing he lifted his hind
toe to scratch it.

And he found that
he actually had hind legs!
Instead of dingy velveteen he
had brown fur, soft and shiny,
his ears twitched by
themselves, and his whiskers
were so long that they
brushed the grass.

He gave one leap and the joy of using those hind legs was so great that he went springing about the turf on them, jumping sideways and whirling round as the others did, and he grew so excited that when at last he did stop to look for the Fairy she had gone.

He was a
Real Rabbit at last,
at home with the
other rabbits.

utumn passed
and Winter,

and in the Spring,
when the days grew warm
and sunny, the Boy went out
to play in the wood behind
the house. And while he
was playing, two rabbits
crept out from the bracken
and peeped at him.
One of them was brown
all over, but the other
had strange markings under

his fur, as though long ago
he had been spotted, and
the spots still showed through.
And about his little soft
nose and his round back eyes
there was something
familiar, so that the Boy
thought to himself:

"Why, he looks
just like my old Bunny
that was lost when I had
scarlet fever!"
But he never knew that
it really was his own Bunny,
come back to look at the
child who had first helped
him to be Real.

About the Author

Margery **Williams Bianco** was born in London in 1881. She was the daughter of a lawyer and scholar who believed children were better educated without formal schooling. As a result, Williams was homeschooled in both England and America, where she moved when she was nine years old. She would alternate living in the two countries for the rest of her life.

Margery Williams's first novel, written for adults, was published when she was only seventeen years old. *The Velveteen Rabbit*, written in 1922, was her first attempt at writing for children. "It was by a sort of accident that *The Velveteen Rabbit* became the beginning of all the stories I have written since," she once said. "By thinking about toys and remembering toys, they suddenly become very much alive. [The story is about] toys I had loved as a little girl—my almost forgotten Tubby, who was the Rabbit, and Old Dobbin, the Skin Horse—and the toys my children had loved."

This edition of *The Velveteen Rabbit* includes the original 1922 artwork by William Nicholson that helped bring to life the Velveteen Rabbit, the Skin Horse and even the nursery Fairy. In keeping with the focus on the world of toys, rabbits and nursery magic, there are no depictions of human beings, not even the Boy who plays such a large role in making the Velveteen Rabbit real.

Unlike the original edition, which was less than forty pages long, the text here is set to highlight the power of Margery Williams's poetic words. It is meant both as an easier reader and to help you think about the profound meaning of what is being said to and by the Velveteen Rabbit. In the style of all great children's stories, there is nothing wasted in *The Velveteen Rabbit,* and every word is as relevant to the lives of adults as it is to the lives of children and toys.

The idea that toys have a real life of their own, both with their human companions and quite apart from them, was integral to the way Margery Williams thought about the world. In fact, her daughter once remarked that her mother always treated their toys as if they were real animals or people. Perhaps that is why *The Velveteen Rabbit* has struck such a chord, and why it continues to be so well loved by children all over the world. As Williams said, "Nothing is easier than to write a story for children; few things are harder, as any writer knows, than to achieve a story that children will really like."

Margery Williams wrote, along with several adult novels, thirty books for children, but none ever achieved the fame of *The Velveteen Rabbit.* She died in 1944 after a three-day illness.